D1524892

DADDIES' GIRL

THEIR BABYDOLL, EPISODE 1

CALISTA JAYNE

Daddies' Girl, Their Babydoll, Episode 1

by Calista Jayne

ABOUT THE BOOK

Calling one man "daddy" is naughty enough—but two?

My creepy ex keeps popping up everywhere I turn.

My apartment is in shambles.

My life is spiraling out of control.

But a steamy encounter with not one but two commanding men shows me that maybe it's time to let someone else—or two someone elses—take care of me.

They have extreme expectations for what it means to be theirs...but after one taste of the pleasure they dole out, I'm hooked. I'll do anything, as long as they'll call me their babydoll.

FOREWORD

Daddies' Girl is an episode (or rather, a collection of episodes) of the serial *Their Babydoll*. It is not a complete story, nor is it meant to be.

This installment does not have a neatly-tied ending, as the story is ongoing. It is one of six collections of episodes.

Daddies' Girl
Daddies' Babydoll
Daddies' Little Angel
Daddies' Princess
Daddies' Sweetheart
Daddies Ever After

Together, these collections make up the entire three-season serial.

I am beyond grateful to my first readers on the serial app where this was first published, who encouraged me, pointed out flaws, begged for more episodes, faster, and made the writing of this book into a truly unique experience.

PROLOGUE

Olivia

The dream is almost too real. Lips trail across my skin, creating a path of heat from my throat, between my breasts, down to my navel. And then lower.

I gasp and reach down to guide the man where I want him, where I *need* him. His lips encircle my clit and he sucks gently before kissing his way down my pussy and licking the slit. His tongue slides in and I moan, helpless against his wicked mouth. He presses a finger inside of me, and then a second one, and I'm writhing against him, chasing my orgasm.

My phone vibrates next to me, waking me up.

Crap. That's hardly fair. I wake with a start and find myself lying half across the rickety desk in my university-assigned art studio. The studio isn't much to look at, but as a senior at San Esteban School of the Arts, having my own studio is something I've earned.

And being surrounded by my own sculptures? It's an amazing feeling.

My phone buzzes again, and I look at the screen.

Daniel: *I'm heading to your place with takeout. Come home soon or I'll eat it all.*

I smile and text him back. *Is it from the taco place I like?*

Daniel: *Nah, I didn't feel like tacos. I got Subathon.*

Olivia: *Okay, thanks.*

I won't be in a rush to get home, then. Subathon sells cheap fast-food sandwiches, and while I don't mind the idea of cheap and fast, Daniel knows very well I got food poisoning last time he picked up dinner there. But if I complain, he'll throw a hissy fit, so I wake up my laptop and try to get back to work. I'm definitely not in a rush to return to the apartment—he can eat both sandwiches, for all I care.

As I stare at the blank document on my laptop's screen, the sculpture behind it captures my attention. *I* made that beautiful thing. It still surprises me, sometimes, to look at it.

The spiraling arches are made of two abstract forms. It's more sensual than I'd originally intended—it reminds me of two lovers in an embrace. Three, actually, because of the shadows formed by the arches. I wonder if the sculpture is responsible for that crazy-hot dream I was in the middle of. Damn, I need to get laid. Maybe I'll get lucky tonight and Daniel won't be passed out in front of the TV when I get home.

Then again, I doubt he could do what that faceless guy in my dreams was doing. Getting head from Daniel is rare, but to be honest, I don't encourage it because he acts like it's a huge favor to me.

Not for the first time, I wonder why we're still together. I wonder if I should break things off.

But then who would I be left with?

———

AN HOUR PASSES. Daniel texts again just as I'm starting a new paragraph on my final project essay. I ignore my phone and try to recapture the thought.

He texts once more, and I glance at my phone.

Daniel: *Where are you?*

Jeez, give me a minute. The sentence in my head is right there, so close to my consciousness. Writing doesn't come easily to me, and I had it—

Daniel: *What the fuck, Olivia? Where are you?*

Giving up on my essay, I text back, *I'm at the studio, trying to write my paper.*

Daniel: *You can do that at the apartment.*

Olivia: *Too many distractions.*

Daniel: *I'll be quiet, promise. Need you here, O.*

Sighing, I pack up my laptop. I should just leave it here in my studio, because I know there isn't the slimmest chance I'll be able to work at my apartment, not with Daniel there, either hovering or watching television. But maybe when he leaves for work in the morning—a cushy, paid internship at his parents' company—I'll get some time to concentrate on my final essay.

As I walk to my car, which is parked on the far side of campus, I'm not thinking about my essay, my sculpture, or my boyfriend. I'm thinking about that dream. I can't remember what the guy looked like or if my dream even gave him a face other than the lips and tongue that lapped at my pussy.

It wasn't just the sexiness of it, either. There was something about the way he licked and kissed me, like it was his life calling. Like he *treasured* me. Like he wanted to take care of me.

But that sort of thing is imaginary. Nobody could care that much.

———

Jaxon

I know it's a dream because in real life, I'm single, and I haven't touched a woman in weeks. But there's a woman in front of me. On her hands and knees. Brown hair. A plump, smackable ass, which I'm currently framing with my hands on her hips as I thrust into her pussy.

Damn, she feels good, her cunt so snug on my cock.

She makes desperate moaning sounds. "More, Daddy, please," she begs.

"I've got you, Babydoll," I say, grunting with the desire to come, but the need to hold back until she finds her own release.

That's new. I don't usually give pet names to my sexual partners right away. They have to earn it, usually after several hook-ups. Maybe I'm dreaming of a long-term relationship, or something with formal parameters. Hell, I don't know. It's a fucking dream and it's stupid to question it.

I glide in and out of her, murmuring soothing nonsense like how hot she is, what a good girl she is to take my big dick so well. The words seem to get her off, because she's moaning louder, and I can feel the rhythmic tightening of her pussy as we fuck. She'll come soon, I bet, but I don't want this miracle dream to end.

I don't want to say goodbye to my new babydoll.

Then Ryder shows up. He's in front of her like magic, kneeling on the bed like I am, his cock out and pumping in and out of her mouth. He wraps her hair around his fist and uses it to guide her movements. Every thrust of his pushes her back on me.

"She's responsive," he says, a smile curling his lips.

"She loves punishment." I point to one of my hand-prints, which has reddened her ass cheek.

"You like to be punished, little girl?" Ryder asks, thrusting harder into her mouth. "If you've been bad, your daddies will hurt you, do you understand? And you might think you like it, but we'll make it hurt a lot."

Her pussy tightens on my cock. Fuck, she's like a piece of heaven, riding me in this dream.

I wake up when I come, and I'm alone in the darkness of my bedroom. Fuck. I haven't had a wet dream since I was a teenager.

And I haven't ached this bad for a woman since before Genevieve.

My nightstand clock tells me it's four in the morning. I don't have to be at Ironwood Security for several hours, but that's the life of a business owner—hours mean fuck-all when you're running the place. If I want to go in at four-thirty in the damn morning, I can go in at four-thirty. If I want to go in at eleven, and stay until nine in the evening, no one will question it.

Well, Ryder would tell me I need to get a fuckin' life, but that's nothing new.

I get into my shower to clean the jizz off my stomach, where most of it landed instead of on my sheets, thankfully. As streams of warm water flow over my head and drip over my back, I close my eyes and lose myself to the feeling of heat and contentment. My mind returns to the brown-haired woman from the dream. For some reason, I wish I'd gotten a better look at her face. All I caught was her profile when she took a breath while sucking off Ryder.

As my thoughts settle on her and her luscious,

curvy ass, my contentment dissipates and turns into an all-consuming need. Before I know it, my dick is hard again. Unbelievable. I take it in my hand, stroke firmly, trying to recall the exact sound of Babydoll's voice while I plunged into her tight hole. In my mind, she moans just as loud and I reach around to run my fingers over her slippery clit. Her pussy's dripping with her arousal and she has to brace her hands on the wall of the shower to keep her balance.

I come again with a shout.

But by the time I'm all dried off and getting into my boxer briefs, the woman's sweet face—in profile, damn it, because I didn't see her straight on in my dream—floats into my head again, and my cock hardens.

Obviously it's time I go out and find a woman to hook up with. Even better if I can convince Ryder to join me. We can each show a woman a good time when we're on our own, but together, bringing a woman pleasure with our cocks and tongues? So much better.

***

Ryder

I wake up late, around seven-thirty. My cabin's quiet—it's why I picked this place next to the lake. So it isn't the city noise pollution that woke me up.

I flip over to my side, feel the drag of sheets over

my dick. It's sensitive now, hard as a fuckin' log between my legs.

The threads of a dream are still lingering in my mind. It was a sex dream, and the only reason I didn't come was something woke me up. Dammit. There were the makings of a good dream, there.

My phone vibrates on the nightstand, and I realize that's what woke me. Fuck. I look down at my texts and see Jaxon has sent me a message. He probably wasn't worried about waking me up, because I'm usually wide awake by six.

Jaxon: *Club tonight?*

I fall back against the pillow and close my eyes. I don't want the club—I want the woman I was dreaming about. All I can recall is...shit, it's gone. I have the feeling of her warm mouth on my cock, and her tongue swirling up the length of it. A glimpse of mischief in her eyes, like she wants me to order her around so she can be a brat.

I love brats. I love to hear their sass, and then their moans when I spank the sass away.

Jaxon: *Don't ignore me, man. I'm not saying we have to marry the first girl we find. It can be casual.*

Flashes of my dream punch through my mind, each one arousing me further. A casual night, sharing a woman's soft, welcoming, and enthusiastically consenting body with my best friend again...yeah. I could get on board with that.

Fuck yeah, I type back.

It's been way too long since we went after a girl together.

––––––

Jaxon

I walk into Club Vice. Not much has changed since I was last here, what, a year ago? Two? It's no surprise the place isn't just surviving, but thriving, because the owner, Margot, is a freaking business genius.

Ryder doesn't seem to be here yet, so I make my way through the crowd and find the last empty seat at the bar. They're in between DJ sets right now, so the music is muted and energy on the dance floor is low.

There are still people dancing, though. The lighting is low—no ridiculous flashing rave-like displays. Club Vice is understated, elegant. It's still a meat market, for sure, but it caters to people with a little more money than the average college student. We're not just looking to hook up, here; we're looking for an experience.

I order a drink and lean against the bar, waiting for Ryder. We usually like to check out available women together and decide who to try to pick up.

A man and woman sit on one side of me, close to the end of the bar. They're bickering loudly over the music, and I'm just about to wonder if the bouncer shouldn't come by and break the two of them up before the woman slams a beer bottle over the man's head or something—and then suddenly they're embracing and practically dry-humping at the bar.

Amused, I watch them for a minute, wondering just how far they're going to take this interlude. His hand is halfway up her dress, quite obviously stroking her pussy, and she's cupping his dick over his pants.

Someone shouts at them to get a room and they break apart, then quickly leave the club.

I finish my drink. As I set it down, I catch sight of two women sitting a few stools down from me—one has blond hair, and the other has dark red hair. The blond one leans back and I catch her friend in profile.

And there she is—it's her. The girl from my dream. Her hair's the wrong color, but that's her profile, exactly.

The word "babydoll" is on my lips already, but I keep it inside.

I flag down the bartender, who's been flirting with the girl's friend. I ask him to send over drinks with my compliments. He smiles at me knowingly. "I overheard the redhead just broke up with an asshole."

Rebound sex. It isn't my usual MO, but if she's happy about the break-up, maybe our time together could be more about celebration than revenge.

My babydoll looks over at me. Is she surprised I sent her a drink? She shouldn't be—she's so fucking gorgeous, it's a wonder she isn't surrounded by drinks sent to her by hopeful assholes like myself.

I debate going over to say hello. Ryder's nowhere in sight, but he'll get here soon. I should wait for him.

A few minutes later, the two women get up to dance.

I watch them for several long moments—and by "them" I mean "Babydoll," because I can't take my eyes off of her. A fierce, possessive feeling overtakes me. I have to make her mine, even if just for one night.

1

Olivia

When Samantha's text comes in, Daniel looks sharply at my phone, his green eyes narrowing. I don't know why it bothers him so much when I receive texts. He's more interested in the basketball game playing on my TV than he is on me.

"Who's texting you?" he asks.

"Samantha."

"Why?" His voice is belligerent, combative. He acts like it's weird for my own friend to text me.

"She wants to hang out." The words are out of my mouth before I've thought them through, and I immediately cringe. Daniel doesn't like Samantha. He hasn't liked any of my friends, actually, to the point that most of them have dropped off my radar—or rather, after

I've said a hundred times that I can't hang out, they've stopped inviting me places.

Samantha is the one last hold-out.

"Well, tell her you can't," Daniel says, turning back to the TV. The glow of it reflects against his sandy brown hair—the product he puts in his hair makes it shiny. He continues, "You're hanging out with me tonight."

I look from him to the TV screen. Yeah, this is real quality time, me and my boyfriend of six months.

"Actually," I say, "let's see what she wants to do. Maybe we can all go somewhere."

He sticks his hand down the front of his sweatpants and scratches his nuts. Classy. "I'm comfy. We'll stay in. I'll take you out somewhere nice tomorrow night, promise."

Samantha texts a second time and my phone buzzes. *Hellooooo. You there?*

"Could she stop it with the texting already?" Daniel snaps.

I fumble with my phone, nearly dropping it in my haste to unlock it and write back to Samantha. Maybe if I'm fast enough, she'll get the hint.

I'll make another excuse. Like I always do. *Staying in tonight, sorry, not feeling great*. The lie pops into my head immediately, like I've been trained to spout it out. It's practically an earworm by this point, an old song I can't stop singing.

As my fingers hover over the keypad, though, I

stop. Why should I stay here with Daniel McScratchyballs?

Why am I even *with* him?

It's almost as if I'm standing outside of my body, looking around at the scene. My living room, which used to be neat, has various piles stacked around it. Piles of Daniel's dirty clothes. Piles of his clean clothes. Piles of dishes he still hasn't taken to the kitchen after I flat-out refused to take them for him.

Beyond the physical evidence that this isn't working out, there's the tension in the air. My fear, mostly. Fear of him getting pissy and broody if someone texts me. Fear of spending an entire evening comforting him when he's butthurt over his team losing.

Fear of never getting out of this relationship.

Holy shit. Why haven't I broken up with this douchebag yet? Is it his looks? I used to find him attractive, and I suppose, objectively, he is, with his thick brown hair and green eyes. But nothing about him does it for me anymore. The only thing I feel when I look at him anymore is tension.

Clenching my phone in my hand, I say, "Daniel, we need to talk."

"What?" He keeps his gaze on the television screen.

"Dammit, Daniel, I'm trying to break up with you. Would you please pay attention?"

He sits up with a grunt and moves his feet to the floor. "Don't be stupid, Olivia. We're perfect together."

"This"—I wave my hands at my messy apartment, and then between him and me—"this is not perfect. This is not together. It's over."

"Wait a second. You don't want to do this without even talking to me first."

"This is me talking."

He shakes his head. "This is you having crazy time. Are you on the rag or something?"

"This is me finally seeing clearly everything that's going on here. Please leave my apartment. It's really over, and I'm not interested in talking things out."

"Olivia. Baby. I love you."

Six months and he never said those words until now. A week ago, I would've been thrilled at this little crumb that said our relationship was progressing right on track. Now, though, I see it as another way he's manipulating me.

Shaking my head, I say, "I'm going out with Samantha. When I get back here, you better be gone."

He stands up and moves toward me, but I whirl around. I grab my purse and I'm out the door, into the hallway. When I close the door to lock it after me, he's standing there, staring. He reaches down wordlessly and scratches his nuts again.

———

Olivia

I take the shot Samantha holds out, then lift it in a salute at the tall, commanding man sitting down the bar from us. He looks too sophisticated for a place like this, too handsome to be legal.

The crowded dance club is teeming with hundreds of people. Most of the women are dressed far sexier than me. Yet he's still looking at me.

Those other women are probably far more single than I am, too.

I'm single, yes. Thankfully so. But I just broke up with Daniel two hours ago. I should be sadder about this, right? And I am sad. Tears even fill my eyes. But they are tears of relief, not regret. The only regret I have is not dumping his ass sooner.

"You doing okay, Olivia?" Samantha asks.

I run a finger underneath my eyes, making sure none of the moisture smears my make-up as I wipe it away. "I'm good."

She leans over and gives me a hug, then turns to face the bar. Flagging down the bartender, she says, "Another round of...whatever it is that the man down there sent us."

The bartender winks. "No problem, chica."

Samantha bats her eyelashes at him. She's a shameless flirt, especially with bartenders. Something about them just does it for her.

I don't know how to tell her how grateful I am that

she texted me tonight. She'd said nothing about Daniel, but the texts had sparked an inner revolution. Now that I'm away from Daniel's influence, I can better see what a bad place I'd been in.

Not only did Samantha spark that inner revolution, she'd also squeezed me into one of her dresses and done my make-up. She is incredible. As if sensing my feelings, she reaches over and squeezes my hand.

"You're the best," I tell her.

"I know," she says simply. "Now, tell me about your final project."

My final art project is a ginormous sculpture, but I haven't shown it to her yet. "It's a big, phallic monstrosity," I say.

She laughs. "It is not."

"I can't wait for you to see it," I say. "It's nearly finished."

"I keep trying to invite myself to your studio…"

"Soon," I say. "I promise."

I risk a peek back down the length of the bar. The man is still sitting there, but he isn't looking at me anymore.

I tell myself I'm not disappointed. My sheets probably still smell like Daniel—strong cologne that can't mask the stench of dirty feet.

"There aren't any cameras around, right?" I ask.

"Olivia. Seriously. No one is paying attention to you. My wig idea was genius, I will not-so-humbly admit, and your make-up makes you unrecognizable. Okay?"

"Okay." I touch one of my eyebrows. Samantha colored them with auburn eyeliner to match the wig, giving my natural medium brown hair and brows a little pop of color.

"Stop touching your face or you'll ruin your make-up," she says, grabbing my wrist.

The bartender brings over our shots and we tap the counter before tossing them back.

"Let's dance," Samantha says, jumping from her stool to do a little shimmy.

A pulsing beat has filled the club. Samantha and I aren't the only two heading out to the floor. Everything is loose and free. Those two shots were exactly what I needed. I resolve to forget the hottie who was parked a few seats down the bar from us, and I lose myself in dancing, instead.

My hips sway with the beat, my feet move, my body twirls. The press of people is sexy, intoxicating as the music. Strong hands grip my waist from behind, moving with my swaying for a few beats before taking control. I can't see the man who holds me, but his hands are warm and they caress my body even while they direct my movements.

Desire pools in my belly. I love being controlled like this—I always have. I used to want Daniel to take more control in the bedroom, but the one time I worked up the nerve to ask, he laughed at me.

When my cheeks heat at the memory, I start to lose the beat of the music. As if sensing my inattention, the man dancing with me yanks me back against him. My body is flush against his, and I feel his package nestled against my ass. The pounding music swallows my gasp.

He smells like citrus and leather. I try to turn, to see his face, but his grip keeps me in place. For some reason, I'm not bothered by this. Samantha is nearby, dancing in a group with some other women and men —including the bartender, who must be done with his shift or on a break. When I catch her attention, her eyes widen and she gives me an approving smile.

My partner lifts one of his hands from my waist and waves to someone else. Then finally, *finally*, he spins me around and I can look up into his face. It's the man from the bar. He's tall, which I had already guessed based on where his cock rested against my upper ass. What I hadn't known was just how handsome he would be. His cheekbones are prominent over a carefully trimmed beard. I can't see the color of his eyes in the dim club, but I can tell they're dark, and heavy-lidded. Bedroom eyes. His hair is dark, also, and cut short.

He takes my hands in his and links them around the back of his neck. It causes my body to move closer to him, and my braless chest mashes against his.

When a second set of hands grabs my waist, I jerk forward into my dance partner. He bends slightly and whispers, "Easy. It's a friend of mine."

I turn my head to see his friend, but all I can glimpse is shaggy dark hair and blazing eyes, either a pale blue or green—I can't tell in the club's lighting.

Sandwiched between two guys—wow. I never would have imagined this at the start of my night. I look for Samantha again, and she's watching me with her mouth wide open.

"Get it, girl!" she calls, her words nearly drowned out by the music.

So I let the men manipulate me, bending my body to their will through that song, and the next. Every slide of hands, every press of their pelvises, every breath against my neck, and I grow more and more feverish with desire. I haven't ever felt so heavy, so ripe and ready.

The guy in front rubs his cheek against mine, his beard abrasive in a way that makes me shiver. The guy behind presses an open-mouthed kiss to the place where my neck meets my shoulder. Liquid desire spirals through my core. My moan is lost in the music, but he must sense it because he tightens his hands on my hips and yanks me against him. His cock is hard, and I rub my ass against him.

Wanton. Lustful. Horny.

The first guy reaches down and touches the place where my hem meets my thighs. He teases the skin there, fingers splaying upward beneath my skirt.

I hardly know myself. I'm ready to fuck two strangers on the dance floor.

2

Olivia

I wonder if it would be too forward of me to suggest we get a room at the hotel one block over. The very idea of speaking what I want causes my stomach to tie itself in knots. I've never been good about taking control. But I want to go somewhere with one of these guys, fuck out all the desire pounding through my core. My pussy has never felt so empty and needy. Surely one of them would say yes? If not both?

I nearly laugh at the thought. Inviting one of them for no-holds-barred sex is one fantasy entirely. Inviting two? I can't even comprehend it.

Then I feel the brush of skin on my inner thigh. My dress has been hiked up slightly in the front, but the guy there is blocking anyone's view.

A voice in my ear asks, "Is this okay?"

And the hand creeps upward. Hot. Confident.

I nod, but I can't believe what I'm about to say. Still, I want this—I want it more than anything. "Yes."

He reaches my folds, which are covered by a flimsy bit of lace, and he pushes my panties aside.

Holy fuck. We're really doing this. I look at the people dancing around us. They don't look our way, absorbed in their own dancing. Then I send my gaze up to the guy in front of me. His focus is intent on where the other guy's hand disappears beneath my skirt.

The second guy's finger slides along my already-wet pussy, and I whimper.

"Fuck," the guy in front of me says, flicking his gaze up to mine.

Music pulses around us, its beat heady and hypnotic. The guy behind me is rubbing against my ass while he fucks me with his fingers. My legs are weak and I hold tight to the arms of the man in front of me. Taken away by the sensation of my impending orgasm, I close my eyes.

The man in front leans close; I can feel his breath on my cheek. "Open your eyes, Babydoll."

One word, *babydoll*, not two. Somehow, I can see the letters in my mind, and they imprint there. I open my eyes, see his gaze clashing against mine. He brings up a hand and wraps it securely around my throat. Not a choke, but tight enough to hold my head in place as he lowers his lips to my mouth.

Citrus explodes over my tongue, and fire. He presses his tongue between my lips—commanding, claiming. I allow him in, kissing him back as if he's the very air I need to breathe.

I'm kissing one man while another one pumps a second finger into my pussy. The heel of his hand rubs against my clit.

I come undone, crying out against the kiss.

They hold me in their arms, and we sway to the music as my aftershocks fade. I want more with them both. Right now. Here, in public, I don't care.

"Good job, Babydoll," the man in front of me says, then kisses my cheek.

The current song ends, and the guy behind me steps away. I crane my neck to look for him, but the guy in front of me touches my chin with a single finger and redirects my gaze toward his.

"I like eye contact," he reminds me in a deep voice that sends ripples of pleasure throughout me.

I'm careful to keep my gaze on his face.

"Good girl," he says.

Another ripple of pleasure, this one more like a wave, cascades within my body. My lips part and I want to kiss him so, so badly. I risk a glance at his mouth. His lips look soft yet firm against his beard. I already know they feel like heaven against my lips, and I want that again.

"Ah, I'd ruin you, Babydoll," he says.

Blinking up at him, I surprise myself when I say, "Maybe I'd like that."

He laughs—the bastard laughs. For some reason, that hurts more than anything else he could have done.

He adds, "You're so cute when you don't know what you're talking about."

Well, that's enough humiliation for one night. Daniel laughed at me—more than once. He always made me feel stupid. I don't need to stay here and let this total stranger make me feel stupid. I step back and look for Samantha.

"Come here, Babydoll," he says, gripping my wrist so I can't walk away.

I shoot him a look that I hope is laden with a combination of disgust and indifference. "My boyfriend is waiting for me."

"Don't insult me with an excuse like that," he says. "I'm sorry for laughing—trust me, it's nothing you did wrong."

Giving him a grumpy look, I pull away from his grasp and fold my arms over my chest.

He smirks. "Be a good girl and take this."

I watch as he pulls a card from his breast pocket, as well as a pen. He scribbles something on the back of the card and hands it to me.

His gaze intent on mine, he says, "If you're ever looking to get ruined—truly ruined—give me a call."

I will never call him. I take the card anyway, vowing to drop it on the floor as soon as he steps away.

But when he leaves, I tuck it into the top of my dress, where the tight fabric holds it in place.

3

Jaxon

It's with regret that I leave her on the dance floor. Ryder took off too fast, but I get it—he doesn't want to get involved.

Still, I can't help but think he acted like a dick. We just danced with the most exquisite woman I've ever laid eyes on, and he takes off immediately after making her come all over his fingers?

I can just imagine him now. *You get too attached, too fast, Jaxon. Remember Genevieve.*

Yeah, I fucking remember Genevieve.

The bouncer waves at me as I leave the club. No, I don't own the place, what kind of cliché do you think I am? But I do come here frequently enough to know some of the staff.

Cool night air caresses my face. I remember her

lips on mine. My cock is thick and heavy. If I'd been standing behind her like Ryder was, I'd have been fucking her in the middle of all those people, no question. And I'd have been fucking her with my cock, not my fingers.

Pulling my phone from my pocket, I call Ryder.

"What?" he says by way of answering.

Rude motherfucker. "You took off rather fast from the club."

"Yeah, well, places to go, work to do."

The sounds of traffic come through my phone; he's talking to me through his speakers while he drives.

"We could have brought her to my place, shown her a good time," I say.

"Nope."

I take the phone from my ear to glare at the screen, as if that will do any good. "What did you just say?"

"I just said *nope*, and I think you fuckin' heard me, asshole."

What the hell? "What got into you?" I ask, all friendliness gone from my voice.

"You know."

"No, I honestly don't. Please, enlighten me, if you can take a few moments from your busy schedule."

Sarcasm isn't the way we usually talk to each other, but he's being a dick.

"You called her *babydoll*," he snarls.

"Ah."

"Yeah, *ah*. It starts with a pet name and then you're

keeping her and falling in love and then it's like Genevieve all over again."

Called it. I look to the night sky, which is blank of stars from the light pollution, and I'm searching for some kind of neon light declaring that I'm a winner. I knew Ryder was going to bring up Genevieve.

The valet brings my car around, and I pass him a tip that makes him stutter, "Thank you," over and over.

I wave at him, climb in the car, and say into my phone, "Just because I gave her a pet name doesn't mean she's Genevieve. Hell, Ryder, I think that woman wrecked you more than she wrecked me, and I was fucking engaged to her."

Silence on the other end of the line.

"Ryder?" I say.

"Gotta go."

The call ends.

Ryder and I have been best friends since college—sharing a dorm room, then an apartment, and now a business. Throughout it all, we found that we were also very good at sharing women. It works for our dominant, kinky sides, and so far, all of our playmates have been more than pleased.

Even Genevieve was pleased, for quite a long time. Until things went sour.

I want to tell Ryder that I think this woman from the club could be different, that if she calls me, I'll drop everything to ruin her as I promised. But that would mean telling him that I gave her my number, and he'll be pissed about that, too.

I hope he gets over it, because it's been far too long since we entertained a woman in bed for more than a weekend. I'm ready for something lasting, something real.

And my palm itches when I think about reddening that babydoll's fine ass.

———

Ryder

I tear up the road in my haste to get out of the city. Gotta put more distance between me and Jaxon and the girl.

The girl especially. She smelled like fucking candy. So sweet, so hot. I only knew one other woman who could embody sexy and sweet so wholly before.

Jaxon's right—Genevieve ruined me. I'm still not over her and I doubt I ever will be, and that's fine. It's easy enough to find a willing woman to join us every now and then. I try to lose myself in recalling our last partner. She was deliciously curvy. I loved the way her ass moved when I smacked it, and her tits had been magnificent, overfilling my palms while I leaned over her from the back and stroked into her ass. She'd been hypersensitive to nipple play, which had been fucking fun.

I wonder how sensitive Babydoll's nipples are. It's too bad I didn't get a chance to touch them, see how much more she'd grind against my cock. Would she say it's too much and try to squirm away? Or would she arch into my pinching attention?

Fuck, how did this turn into a fantasy about the girl from the club? I try to redirect my imagination to the last woman, but as I try to picture her mouth on my cock, it's instead the girl from the club, Jaxon's new babydoll, whose lips I see. It's her tight pussy I smell on my fingers right now. I should've washed my hand, but like a sick motherfucker, I wanted to carry her candy scent a little longer.

I'll clean it away as soon as I get to my cabin retreat.

4

Olivia

"Bye!" I wave to Samantha and her new bartender boy toy in the back seat of the Lyft as they drive off. Then I punch in the door code and enter my building. The doorman is on a break, so I scurry to the elevator and make my way to my floor. The key to my apartment is already in my hand.

For the first time, I'll be going into an empty apartment. I'm buzzed enough to give myself a literal pat on the back as I make my way down the hall. It certainly hadn't been easy telling Daniel to pack up his few things and leave tonight, but I'd done it. I'd stuck up for myself.

And I'd nearly thrown up afterward. Damn, I hated being an adult. Confrontation was the worst.

When I jab my key into the lock, it doesn't turn. Annoying. I try again, reorienting the key.

It still doesn't work.

I look up and down the hall. Am I more than buzzed? Am I drunk? So drunk that I'm trying to open someone else's apartment door? But a glance at the number in front of me confirms this is my place.

I try one more time.

"Fuck," I mutter. In my irritation, I bang my hand against the wall.

The door across from my apartment opens, and my neighbor Seth sticks his bearded face out. "Hey, Olivia. Wow, great wig."

I touch the auburn wig covering my hair, surprised. I'd forgotten I was wearing it.

Guilt settles in my chest, though—Seth battles with insomnia. I shouldn't have been so loud. "I'm so sorry if I woke you."

"Nah, I'm binge-watching a nature documentary." He holds up a mug of tea that smells strongly of chamomile. "But look, the guy came to change your locks an hour ago. Maybe try your new key?"

I mouth the words. Changed my locks. Try a new key.

"Motherfucker!" I yell at my door.

"Whoa, Olivia," Seth says.

"Daniel changed my locks." Squeezing my eyes shut, I try to take a breath, but all I can do is mutter, "Fuck. *Fuck*."

I reach into my purse for my phone. I'll call Samantha and stay with her while I figure out my next move.

The phone's dead. I choke back a sob. This is fine. I'll figure it out.

Seth is watching me, a concerned expression on his face. "Is there anything I can do? I mean, you can't stay here because my mom will flip, but...anything else?"

Seth lives with his mother, who, despite having been told numerous times that her son is gay, believes that he's going to marry me and give her several grand-children.

I sigh. This sucks on so many levels. "Do you have a charger I can borrow?"

He looks at my phone. "Not one that would match that. I only have a landline. You can call whoever you want from it, though. Just keep quiet so you don't wake my mom."

I have exactly zero phone numbers memorized. Zero. Who remembers phone numbers anymore? Not this girl. People used to write them down, back in the day. Sometimes they'd hand them out on business cards—

Wait.

There's one phone number.

Seth's eyes get big as I run a finger down the top of my dress and pull out the gray card the guy handed me in the club.

Jaxon Marsel, it reads. There's no number on the

front, but on the back, I see his handwriting. Bold, no-nonsense. I bet he's the kind of guy who always writes in all-caps.

I also bet he's the kind of guy who can tell me what to do. He'll have a plan for how I should resolve this issue.

He's also the only contact I have.

"Someone gave you their card?" Seth says. "That's old-school. And soooo sexy. Are they hot?"

"He is, yeah," I say.

"Come in, give him a call." Seth beams. "Maybe I'll make popcorn and watch."

I roll my eyes and go into his apartment. I follow him to an ancient rotary phone nestled beneath a pile of papers on the counter. I knew Seth and his mom don't get out much, but damn.

"Does this thing even work?" I ask.

He laughs quietly. "Yep. Do you think you know how to use it?"

"I've seen old movies, sure I know." It only takes me three tries to get the number dialed.

A gruff voice answers immediately. "Jaxon here."

I'm suddenly tongue-tied. "Um..."

"Spit it out, sweetheart, it's two a.m."

I can hear that he's moving around, maybe walking through his apartment. Ha. He doesn't have any old apartment, I'm sure. He has some swanky penthouse in the nicest part of San Esteban.

"I'm sorry to call you," I say. "I just don't know who else to call, and...we met at the club tonight?"

The sounds of movement on the other end of the line stop. "What happened?"

"We...we danced. With your friend."

"No." He gives a little laugh. "I remember that. I mean, what's wrong now? If you're in danger, you should be calling the police, not me."

"This is more of a personal matter," I say, looking over at Seth.

Seth nods and waves at me to continue. Jaxon's silent, waiting for my explanation.

I say, "My ex has locked me out of my apartment. I was hoping for advice, I guess."

"Give me your address."

"I don't know—"

His voice is a growl. "Do you want my help or not, princess?"

In a quiet voice, I recite the address.

"Are you in a safe place?" he asks.

"Yes, I'm in a friend's apartment, but I can't stay here."

As if on cue, Seth's mom calls out, "Seth, darling? Is that the television? Turn it down, please."

"Sure, Mom," he shouts back. To me, he says, "Olivia, sorry, but you gotta go."

"Right."

"Meet me in the lobby," Jaxon says. "*Inside.* I'll be there in ten minutes."

"Got it," I say quietly. "See you soon."

I hang up the phone and stare wide-eyed at Seth. "He's coming here. To get me."

"Seth?" his mom shouts again.

"Shoo," Seth says to me. "Go get your business card hottie. Have wild, kinky sex. Then tell me all about it tomorrow."

I shake my head at him and gather my purse with the dead phone. Maybe Jaxon will have a charger I can use. Just wait until Samantha hears what Daniel did. She'll make immediate plans for eviscerating him.

Before I go, I leave the business card with Seth. It seems safer for some reason. Not that I'm afraid; I just don't want to be totally stupid.

"Thank you," I whisper to Seth, and then head downstairs.

Down in the lobby, everything is quiet. Eerily quiet. The doorman still isn't back from his break, and maybe he fell asleep somewhere. My mother wouldn't be happy to find out that this place's security isn't as legit as she'd wanted; as a congresswoman, she's been very involved in my living situation, opting to supplement the cost of renting an apartment if the security is better.

The lobby is starting to give me the creeps. The sidewalk beyond the big windows is crowded, people bustling around as they usually would on a Saturday night.

Needing the cool outside air and the noise of other

humans, I step through the lobby doors to wait for Jaxon.

A black sports car pulls up minutes later, and Jaxon climbs out from behind the wheel. His dark eyes survey me and an angry frown appears on his face.

"What are you doing out here?" he asks.

"I—I'm waiting for you."

He hurries over to me and takes my hand. "Did I or did I not ask you to wait *inside* the lobby?"

"Now that I recall," I say as he practically drags me to the car, "there was no *asking* about it. Who are you, my dad?"

"That's a lot funnier than you intend it to be," he says, a dark undertone of humor in his voice.

5

Olivia

That makes no freaking sense, but whatever. He opens the passenger door and helps me into the seat.

"Are you going to buckle me up, since I'm so helpless?" I ask.

Immediately, my cheeks grow hot. I, a near stranger to him, am asking for his help in saving my ass from sleeping in my apartment building's hallway. Perhaps I should turn down the snark.

"Sorry," I start to say.

But he's already leaning over me and buckling my seatbelt. His face is close to mine as he does it, and I pull in his citrus and leather scent. This man is so gorgeous. I have no idea why he's helping me. I don't know what I'd expected, maybe that he'd have the number of an emergency locksmith, or know of a hotel where I could stay. But instead, here he is, in the flesh, taking me...somewhere.

My mother would kill me. I'm getting in the car of a stranger. This was a terrible idea. At least I left Jaxon's card with Seth. It seems a flimsy safeguard, but it's something.

He seems to realize this as he gets behind the wheel, and he says, "You can call Detective Baldwin with San Esteban PD. He'll vouch for me. You could post a picture of us together on a social media channel, but that's likely to do more damage to your reputation than save you from something else."

No, no pictures on social media. Despite the fact I'm still in a wig and make-up, I'm not risking it.

"I'm good, thanks," I say.

"You're obviously not good," he says, handing me his phone. "Call your friend and let her know where you're going."

"I don't know her number."

He curses under his breath, and I can't help the sick feeling of shame growing in my gut.

"I'm sorry," I say. "I know I shouldn't have called you, but yours was the only number...I shouldn't have. I probably woke you up."

"You didn't wake me up, Babydoll," he says in a gentler voice.

I wrap my fingers around and around each other,

needing the movement to focus on so I don't fall apart. "I just didn't know what to do."

Softly, he says, "And you called me, and I'm going to help you."

I exhale. This was exactly what I wanted—what I needed. Someone to take charge. It feels seven shades of messed up that I'm throwing myself at the nearest guy to solve my problems, but something about Jaxon makes me feel safe. What I did in the club with him and his friend? I never would've dreamed of that with anyone else. I knew they'd keep me safe and that no one would know what we were doing from the way they shielded my body as we danced.

We pull into a parking garage underneath a building and he parks the car.

"Stay put, and I'll help you out," he says before exiting.

Perfectly capable of leaving a vehicle, I unbuckle the seatbelt and grip the door handle.

He's there already, opening the door and frowning at me. "Babydoll, we need to have a discussion about a few things. Namely, if I tell you to do or not do something, you obey."

"Look, Jaxon, I appreciate the help, but it doesn't mean you get to be my boss."

He grins. "This is going to be fun. Come on, Babydoll."

"Wait a minute," I say,, accepting his hand and

allowing him to pull me from the car. "Why are you helping me, anyway? You could've told me to fuck off."

"I like you," he says simply.

I follow him to an elevator where he punches in a code. The doors open, we step in, and then we're enshrouded in silence. The walls are mirrored and I take in my appearance—my slinky dress from the club, a smudge of lipstick next to the corner of my mouth, the eyeliner much darker than I would normally wear it.

My head is starting to itch from the wig, and the band feels tight. "Who do I call when someone's squatting in my apartment?" I ask.

"The police."

"It's hardly an emergency."

He gives a little laugh. "You do know there's a non-emergency number, right?"

"Yeah," I say slowly. "I just didn't think...ugh, I feel so stupid."

"Nah, you've had a long night, several drinks, the orgasm of your life on the dance floor while sandwiched between two hot men"—he gives me a roguish wink—"and then you came home to whatever domestic dispute is going on. It's hard to make decisions when you're in a situation like that."

We step off the elevator and directly into a penthouse. I can see the city from wall-to-wall windows. This probably isn't the tallest building in San Esteban, but it's damn close. My mother was an attorney who later became a congresswoman, and I've always had enough money. I've attended fundraisers with her and rubbed elbows with aristocrats. But I've never been in an apartment this nice before, and I can't help but gawk. The décor is subtly rich, in grays and blues, with lighting that invites my gaze past the sitting area and to art on the few places of the wall that aren't taken up by floor-to-ceiling windows.

"Can I get you some water?" he asks.

I'm relieved he's not offering me alcohol. I don't think my system could take any more tonight. "Yes, please. And can I use your restroom?"

"First door on the left," he says, pointing to a hallway.

I find the bathroom and am unsurprised to see that it's just as luxurious as the rest of the penthouse. Before I leave it, I pull the wig from my head. My brown hair beneath is smooshed down and kind of bonkers, but the relief of being rid of the wig is worth it. I find a hair elastic in my purse and put my locks up into a bun. The auburn wig doesn't fit in my purse, so I carry it out of the bathroom with me.

Jaxon turns when I emerge from the hallway, two bottles of water in his hands. His jaw drops when he sees me.

"Sorry," I say, "I know, my hair looks crazy."

"No, you just look different, that's all," he says. His dark gaze roves over my body, as if he's wondering what other secrets I'm hiding.

"I promise, my only disguise was the wig. My mother is in politics, so when I want to let loose, I try not to be recognized."

"Do you often want to let loose?" he asks, a strange expression on his face.

"Are you judging me?" I ask. "After you and your friend practically fucked me inside a crowded club?"

"No. Fuck no. Not judging." He holds up his hands, and the water in one of the bottles sloshes. He hands me the other one, which is still capped and sealed. He probably left it sealed so I'd feel more comfortable, and the thoughtfulness makes me soften somewhat.

"Thanks," I say, taking the water.

"I'm just curious about you, that's all. I still don't know your name, Babydoll."

I wink. "I like *Babydoll* just fine, but you can also call me Olivia."

"Olivia." He holds out a hand for me to shake. "I'm Jaxon."

"It's nice to meet you," I say.

He keeps hold of my hand and tugs me a little closer. "Tomorrow, we're going to call the police and figure out how to get your apartment back. Tonight, we should talk."

There's a heat in his eyes—the same heat I'd seen at the club, and I wonder what I've gotten myself into.

"What do you want to talk about?"

"Remember when I gave you my card?" he asks. "I told you to call me if you were looking to get ruined."

"I—this is an extenuating circumstance," I say.

The heat in his eyes fades and he lets go of my hand. "Okay. The second door on the left is the guest room and there's a bed made up already."

I frown up at him. I hadn't expected him to release me quite so easily. My disappointment settles over my shoulders like a heavy shawl. "Thank you."

"You're welcome, Babydoll."

When I turn around and walk to the guest room, I can feel his gaze on my back, and I can't help but put an extra swing in my step.

"You're playing with fire, Babydoll," he drawls, and I hurry to the bedroom without any more flouncing.

Inside, I find a pair of men's sweatpants and t-shirt that he must have gotten out for me to sleep in. I change into them, feeling more naked than before. My tiny club dress covered less skin, but wearing someone else's clothes is surprisingly intimate.

The clothes smell like citrus, but the bed smells like pine, and somehow the two scents work together to pull me into sleep as soon as I close my eyes.

6

Jaxon

At five a.m., I'm still awake. Olivia is sleeping just two rooms away, and every cell in my body yearns to go to her. Does she know she's mine yet? I want her so fucking bad, my dick hasn't calmed down since the club.

But I need to wait until she wants me back, and I don't think she's in that place yet.

Soft whimpering sounds reach my ears, and I sit up to listen better. Is Olivia crying? I'm tempted to go to her, but maybe I should give her space. She indicated that she's not here to let me ruin her. But comforting isn't the same as ruining. At least, it doesn't have to be.

My particular brand of comfort can definitely ruin a woman.

I can control myself, though. If she needs something—whatever it is—I'm going to offer it to her.

I don't want to waste time overthinking it; I go to the guest room. "Olivia?"

She's on her side, eyes closed. Her entire body is curled up tightly, as if she's hiding from something.

"Olivia," I say. "Olivia, you're having a nightmare."

She moans and jerks in her sleep.

"Babydoll, wake up," I say in a louder voice.

Gasping, she opens her eyes. Her body relaxes a fraction, but she remains tense overall.

"You okay?" I give in to the overwhelming desire to comfort her, sitting down on the bed and taking her hand.

"I had a dream that my ex was after me," she says, still breathing hard.

"Is he abusive?" I ask. A primal part of me is already getting dressed, grabbing a baseball bat, and running to her old apartment to kick his ass.

"Not at all, he's just a douche," she says. "Sorry for waking you."

"It's all right," I say. "Do you want me to wait here, Babydoll?"

"Hmm? No, I'll be okay."

I chuckle. "Then you might want to let go of my hand."

She sits up a little and sees where our hands are joined. "Oh, sorry."

But she doesn't let me go.

"I'll stay here, if you want," I say.

She glances quickly at me in the dim light before looking away. "I'd like that."

"Okay." Lying down on top of the sheets next to her, I inhale her sweet scent. Fuck, she even smells like a babydoll, sweetness and candy. I wonder if she likes lollipops, and the thought of her lips closing over candy has my cock back to its rock-hard state.

I try to breathe evenly and eventually calm myself down. Then Olivia scoots closer to me and lays her head on my shoulder.

"Is this okay?" she asks.

"Yes." Inwardly, I'm grumbling. I should be the one asking consent for things. She's already turning me upside down.

Ryder would be furious, and for some reason, that idea makes me smile. Wait until he finds out the woman he finger-fucked in the club is sleeping in the guest room where he usually sleeps when he's in town.

Once Olivia's breathing becomes deep and even, I allow myself to close my eyes. Finally, I fall asleep.

———

I WAKE up lying on my side, a warm breast cupped in my hand and a plump little bottom pressed against my dick. Absently, I rub my boner in the crease of the woman's ass and caress the breast in my palm. My bed partner moans softly and presses her ass harder against my cock.

Yeah, I'm ready to go. I pinch her nipple and listen to her soft gasp before I bring my hand down to her waist.

The sweatpants she's wearing surprise me, because my female partners usually sleep naked or in the cute little nightgowns I buy for them. In the brief moment it takes me to realize this, I wake up fully.

It's Olivia in front of me, the woman I met last night. Her messy bun of brown hair spills across the pillow next to mine, and she's wearing my t-shirt and a pair of my sweats. Her skin seems to glow in the late morning light peeking through the dark curtains. I want to kiss the place on her neck right beneath her ear.

But we haven't talked about doing anything like this. Reluctantly, I let go of her breast and flip over on my back.

"Jaxon?" she asks, spinning around. "I need you."

Words that would normally crush my resolve into dust. "We haven't talked about how this usually goes," I say.

"So you're kinky, I get it," she says. "You want to spank me or something?"

I can't help it, I laugh.

She sits up slightly, bracing her arms on my chest. The indignation on her face is priceless as she says, "You don't have to make fun of me."

"Not making fun of you, Babydoll," I say. "What I want isn't the kind of thing you'd read in a bored housewife's erotic fiction collection."

Wrinkling her nose, she sits all the way up on her knees and stares down at me. A faint blush covers her cheeks and moves down to her neck. "Then what is it you want?"

"I do like giving spankings, to naughty girls who deserve them. But I also like rewarding good little girls who listen to their daddies."

She thinks about that for a moment, and I love the way her forehead wrinkles while she does. "I've heard of this," she finally says. "So you're a daddy dom?"

I shrug. "If you have to put a label on it, yeah, I suppose I am."

I love that she isn't immediately dismissing the idea. It gives me hope that she might be into it.

She considers me with her gray eyes, and her plump lips are slightly pursed.

After a long moment, I ask, "Does some part of this appeal to you?"

"I guess it depends." Her eyes are wide, guileless. "I mean, I don't know much about it."

"That's okay. There's a lot of ways that people do age play. Some parts of it appeal to me—greatly—and other parts don't appeal in the slightest. We could find out what you like, if anything."

She's turned on—I can tell from the way she

squirms slightly, as if she's trying to relieve an empti-
ness in her pussy.

"Is there something you need, Babydoll?" I ask.

"I already told you," she whispers.

"It might be good to tell me again."

"I need you."

"Do you want to try this like I want to do it, or do
you want something vanilla?"

She freezes, like she wasn't expecting to make a
decision. And that's when I know my babydoll was
made for me. She wants cock, but she doesn't want to
say how she gets it.

"You're waiting for me to take control," I say.

Nodding, she looks away.

"Eye contact, please," I remind her.

She snaps her gaze back to mine. The soft gray of
her eyes reminds me of the ocean on a cloudy day.

"If you feel uncomfortable at any time," I say, "you
can use a safe word and everything stops. Your safe
word should be something weird, that someone
wouldn't usually say during sex."

"Like...*bananas*?"

I nod and smile to show her I'm pleased. "That's a
good safe word. Is that what you want to have as
yours?"

"Hmm, no. I think I'd like mine to be *ponies*."

"Sounds good." I sit up and give her my first order.
"Off the bed."

"What? Why?"

"Because I will spank your bottom if you don't do as I say."

She hurries off the bed and stands next to it.

"That nightstand, there. Open the drawer."

She does as I ask, and I enjoy the way her lips part in surprise at the sight of everything stored in there. Lube, condoms, and nipple clamps, if I'm remembering correctly from the last time Ryder and I entertained a woman in this room. Maybe some candy and soft black rope. I wonder if Olivia will like being restrained. I wonder if she'll like spankings. I sure hope so—I can't wait to put my handprints on her ass.

"Take out a condom and put it on my cock," I say, moving to the edge of the bed and planting my feet on the floor.

Her eyes widen, but she hurries to obey.

"Good girl," I say as she opens the foil packet.

I push my pants down enough to reveal my dick, and she rolls the condom over it. Her touch on me is soft and tentative.

"Are you nervous, Babydoll?" I ask.

She shakes her head.

I grab her chin in my hand and look her in the eyes. "Be honest with me. Every time. Are you nervous?"

"A little," she admits.

"Talk to me. Tell me why."

This obviously makes her uncomfortable. I wonder what her sex life was like before, if she isn't used to communicating about her feelings when things start getting intense. It'll be an interesting challenge, teaching her how to discuss her needs and wants.

"I'm worried about disappointing you," she says.

I move my hand from her chin to her neck and bring her head down to mine. After pressing a soft kiss against her mouth, I lean back and whisper, "You have nothing to worry about, then. I'm not going to be disappointed."

"Okay." She nods.

"Now climb onto my lap, Babydoll, and take my cock in your pussy."

7

Olivia

At first I can only stare at Jaxon. Just like that? Sit on his cock?

It's a gorgeous cock, though. I certainly won't mind sitting on it. I've been thinking about doing just that since I woke up to the feeling of it pressed against my ass.

This is crazy. I just met this guy.

"I'm not a patient man, Babydoll."

"Right. Okay."

I start to pull off the t-shirt I'm wearing, but he says, "Leave that on. Just take off the sweats."

"Okay." I slip them off. "Underwear, too?"

"Show me."

The dark timbre of his voice alone could make me wet. I slowly lift the bottom of the shirt up to reveal my plain white thong—the pair of undies I'd had on when I left the apartment after breaking up with Daniel.

"Nice," he says, his dark brown eyes growing darker. "Now take off the panties and get on my dick before I lose my patience."

I quickly slip off the thong and step toward him. This feels awkward, all of a sudden, but I'm committed now. I really, *really* want this. My breasts feel heavy and full, my pussy is slick with need.

His pants aren't all the way down, just far enough that his cock can stick out. I slide over his knees and into his lap.

"Olivia, Babydoll," he says, kissing my cheek. "That's good. Now sit all the way down, and take my cock like a good girl."

Wow, so dirty. Yet I love it. I lower myself down slightly until I can feel his tip at my entrance. He's big, but I'm wet enough. He holds his cock in place and I lower again, my thighs straining.

He's in. Not all the way, just the tip. I can tell this isn't going to be an easy fit, but that's okay.

"You doing all right?" Jaxon asks.

"Mm-hmm."

"Can I help you?"

"Yeah," I say.

He wraps his arms around me. They're strong bands holding me in place, and he slowly lowers me the rest of the way onto his cock. My mouth falls open at the feeling of him inside of me. So big, so hard. My pussy stretches to accommodate him, and I feel him *everywhere*.

"Doing okay?" he asks.

"Yeah. It'll be better once we start moving." I begin to lift off of him.

His arms are tight, so tight I can't lift myself up. "Did I forget to tell you, Babydoll? I just want you to sit here. I don't want you to move."

"I—what? No, you didn't say that. Why?"

I *need* to move. Holding him inside of me like this is torture. My body demands the friction of him moving within, and I'm craving the way I know our pleasure would heighten with the speed of his thrusts. I know how this dance is supposed to go; I've done it countless times with a few different partners.

So why does Jaxon want me to be still?

He keeps me in place and kisses my mouth. The slide of his tongue across my lips is slick, sensuous. I kiss him back, moaning. The need to move is all-encompassing. I can't lift off of his cock to get the friction I so desperately desire, so I wiggle a little from side to side.

"Oh, Babydoll. Don't make me punish you." He smiles, as if he really does want to punish me.

Of course he does.

"Are you a sadist?" I ask.

His smile grows even larger. "Maybe a little."

Annoyed, I resolve not to give him an excuse to punish me. I'll deny him that pleasure because he's denying me the pleasure of bouncing on his dick like I really want to do.

"Oh, so you're a stubborn one," he says, sliding his bearded cheek against mine to whisper in my ear. "I like that."

I give a little huff of exasperation, but it turns into a moan when I feel his cock twitch inside of me.

Ignoring my sounds, he says, "This is called cock-warming. I'll ask you to do this from time to time, because I like the feel of your tight little pussy hugging my cock. If I say, 'Babydoll, warm Daddy's cock,' you'll know what I'm talking about, won't you?"

"Daddy?" I ask.

"Yes, Babydoll?"

That wasn't what I meant. I'd meant the whole *daddy* thing was unexpected, despite having heard the phrase *daddy dom* before. But now I'm starting to get it. Age play. Babydoll. Spankings. Calling him *daddy* goes right along with that.

And I have to admit, the idea isn't repulsive. I wouldn't have thought I'd be into this sort of thing, but it's working for me. I mean, obviously it's working, if I'm sitting in his lap and warming his cock.

But the sensation of him inside of me, not moving, is driving me mad with need.

"I need to move on you," I say.

"You can wait," he says simply.

"No, I really need it."

He grins and kisses my cheek. "I might have something for you, so hang on a sec."

I frown. I'm not going anywhere.

When he reaches toward the open nightstand drawer, it causes our bodies to move slightly. I try to take advantage and wiggle a little more, but he draws his hand back from the nightstand, reaches for my breast, and pinches my nipple through the t-shirt —hard.

"Ow!" I yelp.

"Do *not* move," he says.

I can't help the whimper that comes from my throat. "Okay."

This time when he goes for the drawer, I bite my lip and try to stay still.

He comes back with a piece of candy. "Do you like butterscotch?"

"It's all right," I say.

"Okay. This is a hard candy. You can suck on it, but not chew it. Once it's gone, you can stop warming my cock and I'll give you what you need. Understand?"

"Yes." I nod.

"Yes, *Daddy*."

"Yes, Daddy."

"Good girl." He unwraps the butterscotch and waits until I part my lips, then he slides it into my mouth.

Sugary sweetness coats my tongue. He watches me suck on the candy, then kisses my mouth again. He sweeps his tongue across my lips, then inside. Now we both taste like butterscotch.

Lust gathers where we join, demanding that I rub against him. If I feel the slightest movement against my clit right now, I think I'll come immediately. He wouldn't even have to do any work. Infuriating man.

"You okay, Babydoll?"

"I wish you would just let me come," I say, my voice a whimper.

The candy is about half the size it was. I think of swallowing it and telling him that it got sucked away, but I also have a feeling that somehow, he would know exactly what I'd done.

"Show me your tongue," he says.

I stick it out, cupping the candy in it.

"Good job." Keeping his arms banded around my back, he gives two short thrusts into my pussy.

"Oh fuck," I gasp. So close. So very close.

He stops moving and kisses my lips.

"What did you do that for?" I ask, pouting at him.

"Ah, Olivia. I couldn't resist. Are you done with your candy yet?"

I suck on it furiously, trying to get it down to nothing. When it's just a sliver on my tongue, I show it to him again. He kisses me hard, sucking it into his mouth. Then he lets go of me and lies back on the bed.

"What are you doing?" I ask.

"You finished your candy, Babydoll. Now you can do what you want."

"I want your shirt off," I say.

He pulls it up and over his head, revealing a set of sculpted abs and a wide, hard chest with a subtle sprinkling of hair across it. A fainter trail of hair leads down from his navel to his cock.

I can now see exactly where we join, and every part of me throbs with need and want. I shift up and down experimentally. Sparks of desire shoot throughout my body. Closing my eyes, I move again, a little faster.

"Eye contact, Babydoll," Jaxon says. "Daddy wants to see your eyes when you come."

Oh my gosh, his words. So dirty. I open my eyes, staring directly into his.

All I need is a touch on my clit, and I'll be done. I want to savor the moment, but the whole cock-warming thing got me more than ready and I'm about to explode.

When I start to reach for my clit, Jaxon grabs my hand. "You're ready to come? That's my job."

"Please," I say, fighting against his grasp.

"Oh, Babydoll," he says, holding me tighter. With his other hand, he moves toward my clit. I lift up and down, taking him in and out of me, and he begins to meet me, thrusting in time to my movements.

When he touches my clit, I shatter.

Before I have a chance to recover, he flips us over and begins to stroke furiously within me, powerful thrusts that shake the entire bed. He lifts up the t-shirt I'm wearing and palms my breasts, squeezing the nipples between his fingers. If he were someone else, I might think the pinching was accidental, but I'm starting to understand Jaxon. He wants to dominate me thoroughly.

And I want to let him.

Another orgasm builds he continues to fuck me. I grab his shoulders, hanging on tight because this climax just might be the end of me—it grows more and more powerful and electric, like my nerve endings are going to fry.

"Come again for me, Babydoll," he says. "Eyes on me."

The words, his tone, the steely, dominating look in his deep brown eyes, the thrusting of his cock, the pinch on my nipples—all of it comes together to throw me over the edge of expectation and into ecstasy.

I cry out and he kisses me hard, muffling my cries with his mouth. His eyes never leave mine, and then he tenses up, going still inside me except for the telltale twitching of his cock as he comes.

8

Jaxon

I don't want to let go of her. Her body is languid, pliant beneath mine, and she smells sweet like butterscotch. I want to crawl down her body and taste her pussy until she's begging me for release again, but we have work to do.

"So your ex is squatting in your apartment?" I say, rolling off of her and removing the condom. I go into the attached bathroom and dispose of the rubber, then return to the guest room.

"That's my guess," she says. "I don't know why else he'd change the locks."

"Just to spite you," I say, "although I don't know him, so I can't guess what he'd do."

She slides off the bed and bends down to pick up her thong, then grimaces.

"Panties too wet to put back on?" I ask.

"Yeah." She shrugs and starts to step into them anyway.

"Go without," I say.

I fucking love the way her gray eyes widen and a blush tinges her cheeks when I surprise her like that. It makes me want to keep doing it.

"Do you want to tell me what to wear, too?" she asks in a snotty voice.

Oh, I need to have words with her. Advancing toward her, I make my voice low and controlled. "Lose the attitude, Babydoll. And listen closely."

She gasps when I press her up against the wall, holding her in place with my hips. My dick is already semi hard again, just from dominating her like this. Fuck, I want nothing more than to hole up in this guest room for two weeks and really show her what it would mean to be my babydoll.

As soon as we resolve this issue with her squatter ex, that's exactly what we'll do.

"Are you listening?" I ask.

"Yes," she whispers.

"Yes, what?"

She makes a soft little whimper. "Yes, Daddy."

"Good girl. You should feel free to act the brat with me all you want, but when you do, you should expect punishment. And if you think punishment sounds fun, then you haven't seen my particular brand of punishment. It's filthy and painful. Remember what I said last night, about what would happen if you called me?"

"That...that you'd ruin me."

I nod. "That's right."

Her breathing is rapid, her breasts nearly touching my chest. Snaking one hand up under her t-shirt, I find her breast and lightly pinch the nipple.

She gasps and closes her eyes. "Yes."

Then I pinch harder.

Her eyes snap open, big gray oceans. She blinks back tears and says, "Ow, ow, ow."

I don't let go, wanting to help her get my point. Instead, I watch her carefully, waiting to see when the pain morphs into pleasure.

It happens quickly, which pleases me greatly. She begins to squirm.

When I let her go, she moves forward, following my hand, as if asking for more punishment to her nipple.

I shake my head, then pick up her thong. "That's all, Babydoll. Time to get dressed. You can wear whatever you want, as long as it doesn't include this thong. It's way too grown-up for a babydoll's panties."

Wordlessly, she puts on her dress from last night. I make no secret of checking out her body as she pulls it over her curves. When she struggles with the zipper, I say, "Come here. Daddy will help."

She pads over. I can tell all the daddy stuff is new to

her, but she surprisingly doesn't balk. Most women new to the scene seem to feel awkward or unsure. Olivia takes to it naturally.

We would get along so great. Fuck Ryder and his stupid doomsday predictions. Olivia is special, and it isn't just because I gave her a pet name on the dance floor. I inhale her sweet scent mingled with the scents of fucking that linger in the air.

Filthy. Sweet.

My cock twitches. I briefly entertain the fantasy of pushing her to her knees, feeding my dick into her mouth, watching her lips wrap around me. But we have a chore to do. I zip up her little slip of a dress then trace the top over the curves of her breasts.

"Daddy," she says. Her voice is soft, just like her skin.

"Time to go," I say abruptly. Standing in this room with her is too much of a temptation.

Ryder

I fucking hate the city. It's full of people. Desperate people—and I don't just mean the poor or the people who don't have homes. The rich people are some of the most desperate people I've ever met. They're desperate for more money, more power, more admiration.

I should know, because I'm one of them. Fuck.

This cynicism isn't like me. Nor is the self-hatred. But I haven't been able to sleep since going to that club and finger-fucking the most exquisite woman I've ever laid eyes on. She smelled like cotton candy and licorice, and her pussy gripped my fingers like a tight little vise, fluttering over me in a way that had my dick damn near exploding in my pants.

If only Jax hadn't given her his card. If he hadn't done that, I could have let her fall back into the sea of anonymous women. I could have let go of any twisted fantasy involving her calling him and asking to hook up again. I could have forgotten all about her.

I catch my reflection in the café windows as I walk up to it. I look pissed. No wonder, because I'm lying to myself. Dishonesty pisses me off, especially when I know better.

"Hi, Ryder," the barista says when I step up to the counter.

"Felicity, hey. How's it going?"

"Good, good." She winks and takes my order. "I saw you at Vice last night. Looked like you were having fun."

While I stuff some bills in the tip jar, I give her a look because I can see where this is going. "That's all it was. A good time at the club. And how are you even awake and looking so hot this morning? You were still serving drinks when I left."

"Have to pay for med school somehow," she says.

She tries to push my generous tip back in my hand, but I refuse to take it.

"Med school," I say. "One of these days you'll be saving my ass in the ER."

"Thanks, Ryder." She tucks the bills into the jar.

I wish I could do more for her—she's been serving coffee nearly every morning at this little corner café since I moved to this godforsaken city. But she won't take what she views as charity. The least I can do is chat with her and tip well every day.

My coffee pleasantly burns as it goes down my throat. I live for this moment every morning. The only better wake-up is to a fine ass pressed against my cock. I can remember one ass in particular, how tight it was against me last night as we danced.

I should go back to the cabin. Jerk off again. But Jaxon wants me here for the business, so I drove back, and now I'm cranky as fuck.

The drive to the office is quiet because it's still pretty early, and a Saturday. I wonder what Jaxon has in store for us today. Some kind of high-profile client, he'd said. He wanted me to work up the schematics for monitoring their property, then he wanted to go over them together, search for weaknesses. We could make any number of our team members do this kind of work, but for special cases, Jaxon prefers a more hands-on approach.

As I park the car, I see an auburn-haired woman

stepping into the elevator. I practically trip in my haste to reach her, then realize, too late, that it wasn't the babydoll from the club.

I really need to get laid so I can fuck this nonsense out of my system.

9

Olivia

The last thing in the world that I want to do is face Daniel. Talk about a buzz-kill. But Jaxon drives us back to my apartment building and marches me past the doorman and into the elevator.

I'm totally doing the slut strut, wearing a club dress early on a Saturday morning, and normally I might feel self-conscious. But not today, not with Jaxon at my side, looking tall and forbidding.

I lead him down my hallway and up to my apartment door, then point to it.

"Knock on the door," he says. "Ask to talk."

When this is over, somehow I'll have to tell Jaxon how grateful I am that he's taking charge like this, telling me what to do. I know this is something I need to learn to do on my own, but right now? I need it. I need his instruction and his domineering presence.

Knocking on the door, I say, "Daniel? Let me in—we need to talk."

Nothing happens, no sound of movement or anything inside, not even a "fuck you, bitch," like he'd muttered at me when I left for the club last night.

I never should have left him in my place to pack his things. Too late, I realize how stupid that was.

"Daniel," I say more forcefully, and knock harder. "Let's talk. Open the door."

When he doesn't answer, I try the knob even though I know it will be locked.

It isn't locked.

Surprised, I push open the door.

"Wait," Jaxon says, sidling past me to step inside.

I don't know how long I'm expected to wait, but it's my damn apartment, so I push the door open wider and step inside after Jaxon.

The place is trashed. Clothes, furniture, papers, food, and books have been thrown everywhere. Daniel wasn't looking for something, and it doesn't seem like this was done by burglars or anything like that. No, he was purposefully trying to destroy every single thing that I own.

It is all completely, utterly wrecked.

And it smells like shit and piss.

Gagging, I turn around and go back into the hallway.

Jaxon follows me, already dialing a number on his phone. "Yeah," he says, "I need to report an incident. If we could talk with Detective Baldwin, that would be perfect."

———

Olivia

Two hours later, we're done talking with Jaxon's police officer friend, Carl Baldwin. Jaxon and I look at each other outside of the station, blinking in the bright midday light. I'm still wearing last night's dress, and no underwear because Jaxon pocketed my thong before we left his place. It feels strangely erotic knowing he's holding my panties in his pocket while my pussy is bare.

The reason I didn't get any clothes from my apartment was that Daniel had taken every single item from my dresser and closet, thrown it into a pile, and pissed all over it.

I rub my hands over my arms, shivering despite the warm weather.

"New clothes," Jaxon says. "But first, I have to make a call."

Pointing to the bottom of the steps in front of us, I say, "I'll wait over there."

"You'll do no such thing, Babydoll," he says, grabbing my upper arm and tugging me close to his body. "I want you next to me."

The tightness in my chest loosens—it's nice to feel protected and wanted, especially after all the horrible things I had to catalogue in my apartment.

Jaxon takes out his phone and makes a call. "Yeah, about that."

There's a pause while the other person speaks.

"I can't make it today, something came up. I know. So go back to your cabin or wherever. The team can handle the schematics.... No, I wouldn't be doing this for a piece of ass, dickhead. It's important.... Yeah, fuck you, too."

Despite the angry words, he's smiling when he ends the call and slides the phone back in his pocket.

At my questioning look, he says, "Colleague. Friend. Asshole. That's Ryder."

I laugh and slide my hand into his outstretched one, and we walk to his car, which is parked down the block.

Halfway there, I stop suddenly.

"What is it?" Jaxon asks.

"My apartment," I say. "I can't go back. Shit." My mind is whirling. I can't move in with my mom. For one thing, she lives an hour away, and I have classes. For another, she doesn't want me around. Samantha would be the obvious choice, but she's already got four roommates in a three-bedroom apartment—two of them share a room, and one sleeps in the living room. There isn't even a couch for me to crash on.

"I'll help you," Jaxon says simply.

"You barely know me." I'm mentally going through my list of friends, but Samantha's pretty much it. I haven't been close to anyone else, partly because soon after starting the art program, I met Daniel, and all of my time was spent with him.

Maybe I could sleep in my art studio. Bring in a sleeping bag. It would be great for actually finishing my final project.

"Doesn't matter how well I know you," Jaxon says. "I'm in a position to help you, and so I will."

"What are you saying?" I ask. "Do you have an extra apartment somewhere?"

"No. You can stay with me."

This is way, *way* too fast. "I don't think so. That's a terrible idea."

"Why?"

"Because we've had sex. We just met last night. We don't even know each other."

"I know your spirit, Olivia," he says, his eyes on mine. "I think this is the best idea I've ever had. And I've had a lot of good ideas. I'm very...creative."

Of course he would have to make this conversation sexy. He's unbelievable. And as much as I wanted him to take charge earlier, I realize I need to set some limits. Right now, right here.

"Fine," I say, hardly believing the word as it leaves my mouth. "Fine. I'll stay with you, in your guest room. But on one condition—we have to stop sleeping together."

He raises his eyebrows, and his chocolate brown eyes are wide in disbelief. "Well, that doesn't make any sense."

"Yes, it does. I'm paying rent, and I'm not taking hand-outs. I have money. Or rather, my mom has a little. But I'm also not mixing...um...sexytimes with our living arrangement."

Subtly shaking his head, he says, "All right, Baby-doll. You call the shots. But if you change your mind, well, you'll know where my bed is. And I'll be lying in it, waiting for you."

10

Jaxon

The trunk of my car is stuffed full of clothes for Olivia. She was stubborn and wouldn't let me pay for them, claiming she has plenty of money. From the way she blinked in surprise at one of the totals, she doesn't have as "plenty" as she thought.

"Okay, one more stop," I say, steering us down the block.

"I have all I need," she argues, resisting the way I guide her along with my hand on her back.

"Maybe so," I say, "but I want to buy you some things, and—"

"And no." She twists away from my hand.

"And yes."

"What do you think are you, my sugar daddy?" she asks, staring hard at me.

I laugh. "Trust me—my brand of *daddy* doesn't come with much sugar."

"We're not doing any of that sexy stuff," she says. "Remember?"

I look up and down the crowded city street, frowning. She did mention something like that. Our chemistry is so good, I don't think any sort of distance between us will last, and that's why I keep forgetting. Or maybe it's sheer stubbornness on my part—I want to believe that she'll be warming my cock again tonight and I'll be driving her wild, making her wait for the fucking.

"Yes, I remember," I finally say. "We need to eat, though. Can I take you to dinner—*as friends*? In a friendly way? Or do you want to take it down a notch and simply be roommates? Because roommates eat together sometimes, too."

Pursing her lips, she says, "I suppose we can be friends."

She's so fucking cute when she thinks she's in charge.

———

Ryder

A hundred bucks says Jaxon's spending the day with the chick from the club last night. If I'm wrong, I'll buy him a bottle of his favorite whiskey.

He's not going to come right out and tell me, though. So in order to figure out whether I'm right or wrong, it means I have to do a little recon.

I start by swinging by his place. I use the code for the penthouse suite and let myself in. I sleep here almost as much as he does, so it's not as if I'm breaching his privacy.

The living room is empty and all is silent, but I take a look around.

The guest room, which is where I usually crash when I stay here, has rumpled sheets and it smells like sex. Not just any sex. Sweet babydoll sex.

Motherfucker. I knew it.

No whiskey for Jaxon. In fact, he should be giving *me* whiskey. I go to his liquor cabinet, pull down the half of a bottle that remains of his favorite brand. Then I find a pen and notepad in one of the kitchen drawers. I write, *I made a bet with myself that if you weren't with "Babydoll," I'd buy you a bottle. Looks like I was right, though, and you are with her. The whiskey's mine, asshole.*

Then I prop the message up in the liquor cabinet where his bottle had been sitting.

I go back into the guest room, take a swig of whiskey, and inhale. Candied sweetness. My dick is as hard as a fucking tire iron. She smells so damn good. I remember how her pussy felt on my fingers, and I'm imagining how it felt to Jaxon when she was on Jaxon's cock. While he's pounding into her, maybe she'll take me in her mouth.

Fuck it. I take another swig of whiskey, then set down the bottle. I unfasten my pants, take out my dick, and fist it while I stare at the rumpled sheets. I'm imagining her on those sheets on her hands and knees, wearing a sweet little nightie, something girlie like what Jaxon would buy for her. My red handprint would be on her ass because I'd have found some reason or another to give her a spanking.

Jerking myself off to the vision, I breathe in her sweet scent. And when I come in my hand, I say one word. "Babydoll."

———

Olivia

I don't know what Jaxon's game plan is, but he is pulling out all the stops. The restaurant isn't fancy as far as dress code, which is a good thing because my shopping trip for essentials did not include an evening gown. But it's one of the most difficult places to get into in San Esteban.

I'm wearing a deep purple wrap dress that looks professional and sexy all at once. It was my favorite purchase today, and it'll be perfect for my final project presentation, which is coming up in two weeks.

Thank heavens my apartment wasn't big enough for doing anything other than sketching out my sculptures. Those are safe in the university's art building. As a senior, I have my own mini studio.

As Jaxon and I walk into the restaurant, he doesn't put his hand on my lower back like he'd been doing before. He doesn't send me flirty little smiles. He doesn't call me *babydoll*.

And...I kind of don't like this.

"Something wrong?" Jaxon asks as I push food around on my plate.

"Do you mean other than the fact that my ex trashed my apartment and did some unspeakable things to my belongings?"

Anger flashes in his eyes, but it's gone in a second. He nods. "Yes, other than that."

"No, everything's peachy other than that."

He gives me an evaluating look, as if trying to decide what I'm hiding from him, if anything, then nods in satisfaction. "Okay, Olivia, if you say so. Tell me about your work."

"My work? Oh. I'm a student."

"Grad school?"

"Undergrad."

"Shit, how old are you?"

I smirk. "I'm about to turn twenty-two. Is that too young for you, old man?"

"Be careful, Olivia," he says, his voice rougher than it was a moment ago. "You're playing with fire."

"Sorry," I say. My skin feels as if I just got very close

to that proverbial fire. I take a giant gulp of ice water, hoping to cool off. It almost works.

We talk about my art, and it's crazy the kinds of questions he asks—like he actually knows about art and cares about it. He tells me a little about his firm, Ironwood Security. It's all I can do not to make a dick joke about "Ironwood."

He calls for the check and waves me off when I reach for my purse. "My treat," he says. "As your friend."

The words come out of his mouth casually, but then they squat between us like ugly little monsters. He's not happy that I put a stop on our bedroom adventures. I'm not exactly thrilled, either, but if he's renting a room to me in his fine-ass penthouse, I don't want to screw things up by getting involved.

His particular brand of kink scares me. Not because it's too dark or too dangerous or too sinfully sexy. But because I can easily see myself getting pulled in. Not just for a fling, but for life.

Our ride back to the penthouse is quiet. I watch the city streets go by, appreciating the way the lines and the colors have shifted and changed with shadows over the course of the day.

When we get back to the penthouse, Jaxon helps me carry the bags to the guest room. All I can think about is what happened between us the last time we were in here. I stare at the messy bed, thinking of how he'd lain on his back, letting me fuck him as fast or as slow as I'd wanted. I think about the bite of pain as he'd pinched my nipples, and the way the pain had quickly transformed to liquid warmth spreading through my body, concentrating at my core.

A smile plays on his lips now, as he stares at me. It's as if he knows exactly what's going through my mind.

"Do you want something to drink?" he asks, walking back out of the room.

Damn him and his sexy ass.

"No, thanks," I say, but I follow him out.

He moves to a cabinet filled with gleaming bottles. Plucking a notepad out of it, he chuckles softly.

"What is it?" I ask.

"My business partner came by while we were out, stole my whiskey."

He doesn't seem that upset about it, so it must not be like the situation I had with Daniel.

"I need to let him know I've rented out his bedroom."

It takes a moment for the words to sink in. "Wait, I didn't know I'd be ousting someone else when I agreed to stay here. I can find another place—"

"I have two extra bedrooms, Olivia," he says. "Ryder can sleep in the other one."

"Or I can sleep in the other one," I offer. "I hate the idea of kicking someone out of their own room."

He shakes his head. "He just crashes here a lot. Most nights, actually. But he has his own place outside of the city."

"Should I move anything of his out of there before I go to sleep?" I ask. Like, perhaps, his condoms, lube, candy, and what looked like rope and some jewelry.

"No, you can leave it." Jaxon's voice is smug.

He thinks I'm going to cave. He thinks the two of us might be needing those items again.

He is oh, so very wrong.

11

Olivia

I wake up alone in my bed on Sunday. The difference from yesterday causes a veil of loneliness to creep over me, more stifling than the down comforter pulled up to my waist.

The memory of yesterday morning sparkles in my mind like a forbidden gem. I reach for it and allow snippets to flash through my head. My core hums with need.

The bedroom door is closed, so I reach for the waistband of my underwear and slide my hand inside, my fingers gently playing over my clit. I'm already so wet, just with the thoughts of yesterday morning. Warming Daddy's—no, *Jaxon's*—cock. The way he'd made me wait, how I had thought I would explode with desire. The taste of butterscotch on my tongue, the taste of his kiss against my mouth. The way he'd filled me, so fully and completely. His strong arms wrapped around me, holding me in place. I'd felt safe. Cherished. Owned.

I move my fingers faster over my clit, wishing so hard I had his cock inside of me right now. I focus on that, on how he felt inside of me, and I use my other hand to pinch one of my nipples—hard, just the way he did it.

Then I explode, arching upward before falling back and settling against the bed once more.

Fucking hell. If thoughts of what we did before can get me off that quickly, just imagine what could happen if I had the real thing again.

After my heart rate slows down, I climb out of bed and take a shower, hoping to wash away the lustful thoughts.

The attempt is not at all successful.

When I finally emerge from the bedroom, with wet hair and in new clothes, Jaxon is in the kitchen. He, too, is freshly showered, and he looks scrumptious in a pair of gray slacks and a black button-down shirt.

"Good morning, Olivia," he says.

How can three words from him make me feel wet and needy all over again? I should turn right back around, climb into my bed, and have another round with myself. Instead, I clear my throat and say, "Good morning, Jaxon."

"I made some extra smoothie in case you want some."

"Oh, I usually just have a coffee," I say.

He purses his lips, like that isn't a good response, and for some crazy reason, I want to please him. Not just impress him because he's hot and he's my new roommate and I just had sex with him yesterday, but there's an achy spot inside of me that will only be soothed with his approval.

"If there's extra, though, I'd love to try it."

"Of course." He doesn't smile, but he quickly pours a light green concoction from the blender into a pint glass. Handing the glass to me, he says, "Bon appétit."

"Thanks." I take a sip. It's sweet and tart, not bad at all.

"What's on your agenda for today?" he asks, taking a sip of his own smoothie.

"I'll head to school and work in my studio, put the finishing touches on my sculptures and work on my presentation."

"Good," he says. "I have to head into the office. I'll drop you off."

"Oh, is your office close to the San Esteban School of the Arts?"

"Close enough." He smirks.

Meaning, it isn't close at all, but he's going to drive me around anyway. "You don't have to take care of me, you know."

"I don't know if I told you," he says, "but my work is

in the security sector. Personal security. And I didn't like the look of what that asshole did to your apartment. So if you don't mind humoring me, I'd like to be as involved as you'll let me in getting you to and from school."

All traces of flirtation are gone. He's not doing this to get in my pants again; he's doing it because he cares and he's taking Daniel's vandalism seriously.

"Thank you," I say, meaning it and hoping my sincerity shows.

Maybe we'll really succeed at being friends and roommates, and not lovers.

A small voice in my head asks, *But why can't we be all three?*

————

WHEN I UNLOCK the door to my studio space and step inside, I take a deep breath and exhale. This room is my happy place, full of everything I need to create my art.

My mother might not love my pursuit of this degree, thinking it frivolous, but I'm damn good at what I do. The abstract lines and shapes of my sculptures make sense to me in a way that nothing else ever will.

I circle the largest one, which rests on a big crate in the center of the room. The glaze shines beautifully. I knew this piece would turn out well, that I'd applied every different aspect with care and attention. But seeing it here, a finished sculpture that seems to undulate with its own beauty and power, surprises me. Did I really create this? The clay arches and spirals around, and the celadon on the underside contrasts beautifully with the copper coloring above.

Creating this piece was hard, but fun.

Sitting down to write about it is just going to be hard.

Still, my presentation is two weeks away, so it's best to get it done. I pull my laptop from my messenger bag —grateful, once again, that I stored it here instead of in my apartment. Finding a floor cushion in the corner, I drag it in front of the window so the natural light will illuminate the sculpture. While the laptop whirs to life, I stare thoughtfully at the sculpture in the middle of the room.

It doesn't even have a name. Not yet. I'm not sure what to call it.

The spiraling arches are made of two abstract forms. The resulting intertwined piece is sensual— more sensual than I'd originally intended. Still, I can't deny that the sensuality of the piece is a huge part of its power. It draws the eye.

Looking down at my laptop, I try to put those feelings into words. Somehow, I need to convey to my senior committee the reasoning behind my creation, and where I think it succeeds, where it fails.

I'm midway through a sentence about how I struggled with getting the glaze right when a prickly feeling skitters down my back. I shrug, trying to dispel it so I can remember the rest of the sentence that I was trying to write.

The feeling doesn't go away; instead, it intensifies. I pull one of the hair sticks from my bun and use it to scratch my back, but that doesn't help. Irritated, I lose my focus entirely on the laptop and frown. It's only then that I focus on what the skittery, itchy feeling is telling me.

I'm being watched.

I whirl around, hoping to catch the person in the act. But the school quad out the window behind me is full of students studying, either lying in the grass or beneath the shade of several large oaks that dot the campus. Nobody seems specifically focused on me.

Laughing to myself for my paranoia, I return to the laptop.

But I can't shake the feeling.

If there were curtains or blinds over the windows, I'd sacrifice the natural sunlight and pull them just to dispel this weird feeling. But there isn't anything I can use.

Totally creeped out, I grab my phone. I'd been able to charge it at Jaxon's, thankfully.

The only person I want to talk to right now is Jaxon. I want to hear his deep voice and let it ground me to reality. Although my heart's pounding faster than usual, I dial his number.

"Hey," he says warmly.

"Hi, it's Olivia."

"I know, Babydoll. You okay?"

Ignoring the fact that he called me *babydoll* again, I say, "Yeah. Just wanted to…"

Then I stop. Because that's a lie. I am over-the-top freaked out.

"I'm freaked out," I say.

"What's going on?"

"I know it's stupid, but I feel like someone's watching me."

There's no pause. He just says, "I'll be right there."

"Wait, you don't have to—"

"What building, which room?"

"Cassiopeia. Room twelve. But really, Jaxon, it isn't necessary—"

But the line is dead. He's on his way.

I keep my phone in my hand. His urgency has me even more freaked out for some reason. If he's taking this so seriously, maybe I should, too.

A knock on the door makes me jump. He couldn't be here already.

"Olivia? You there?" It's Samantha's voice.

"Yeah, come in," I say. Thank goodness—company.

"I know you're trying to work," she says, sashaying through the door, "but I have *got* to tell you about Bartender Boy."

Taking in my face, she stops.

"You okay?"

I nod. "I think so. I was just getting freaked out. But I'm fine now."

"Okay, because listen. Ben the Bartender Boy is hot AF, and he's already called me back and asked to see me again!"

"That's awesome," I say, and I mean it. She's had a long string of duds. If Ben the bartender is even half as great as she thinks he is right now, that'll make him a hundred times better than her last boyfriend.

She regales me with the tale of her exploits with Ben, sharing more details than I really need, but that's her way. We analyze Ben's likelihood of being "the one," because despite Samantha's relentless search of her next orgasm, she really does want to find the one guy to rule them all.

And then the door bangs open and Jaxon's standing there, fists clenched, looking around the room like he's ready to tear someone apart.

12

Olivia

Samantha squeaks, hand flying to her mouth, then she looks at me with wide eyes.

I clear my throat. "Samantha, meet Jaxon. Jaxon, Samantha."

"I remember you from the club," Samantha says, walking over to shake his hand. Then she turns to me and gives me the stink-eye, the one that says *you better explain yourself young lady and you better do it soon.*

I wince, but Jaxon laughs.

"I don't know if Olivia told you," he says, "but she had a minor problem getting into her apartment."

"We hadn't gotten to that yet," I say, looking at Samantha. "Daniel locked me out while he completely trashed the place. My phone battery was dead and

Jaxon here had given me his card. His was the only phone number I had."

"I see," she says, flicking her gaze between Jaxon and me.

Jaxon's face is impassive as he moves to the window and looks outside—not at the people relaxing on the quad, but at the ground immediately on the other side of the building. He frowns.

"Olivia, if you're ready to go, I can take you home. If you want to stay out longer, I only ask that you let me call a few of my men to be on security detail."

"Security detail? What?" Samantha squawks.

Jaxon clenches his jaw—I can see the ripple of movement behind the beard on his cheeks. "I believe her ex's behavior is more than just a violation of her property. He—or someone else—is violating her privacy, as well."

"What are you talking about?" I ask.

Now that he's here, I'm brave enough to go to the window again and look out. Samantha comes with me.

Jaxon points down at the ground, where footprints are indented firmly into the soft earth. Samantha gasps, but I'm too shocked to react.

Then he raises his finger and points to something else—a tiny camera affixed to the corner of the windowsill.

———

Ryder

When the text comes from Jaxon, I'm not surprised. I stole his whiskey, after all, and no doubt after a long day, he'd gone straight for the bottle for his customary glass before bed. So I'm ready for anger.

I'm not ready for that anger to be directed at an outside threat. I'm not ready to read the subtext of fear in his words.

Some asshole is stalking Babydoll.

And I'm definitely not ready for the pulse of rage that washes through me when I comprehend the message. Some asshole is stalking our girl? I'll fucking rip him apart. Fucker better be ready for pain, because I will dish it out.

Then I realize, I'm just as possessive of her as Jaxon is.

In my mind just now, I called her *our girl*.

Fuck. I slam my hand down on my desk and spin to face the office windows. The city is lit up for Saturday night—swanky clubs with subtle lighting, bass pounding out rhythms through the sidewalks, a carnival of carnal desires.

I turn back to the desk and pick up my phone so I can respond to Jaxon. Chest heaving, I type out, *I'll work up a security plan. Where does she live?*

His response is immediate. *At the moment, she lives with us.*

He's got to be kidding.

Fuck it. I text back, *I'm coming over*.

———

Olivia

Jaxon grimaces at his phone and looks up. I quickly return to looking at the book open in front of me. It's an art history book I found on his shelves, and I haven't read it before. It isn't a super comprehensive treatment of the topic, but I'm mostly staring at the images, anyway.

"What's up, Olivia?" Jaxon asks.

"Just looking at your book. I didn't know you were into art."

"It was my mother's," he says. "She taught art history at the university."

"Taught?" I ask.

"She passed two years ago. Cancer."

"Fuck cancer," I say automatically.

"Did you lose someone, too?" he asks.

"My dad. I don't remember him—I was only three."

He nods. "Fuck cancer."

I allow my gaze to linger on his face—his strong jaw, decorated in the neatly-trimmed beard that I long to rub my hand over. His dark eyes, boring into mine. The slight smile on his lips, the one that says he knows I want him.

The smile falls, and he says, "I should give you a

head's-up. My buddy Ryder is coming by. He's a bit of a grouch."

"I can deal with grouches, no problem," I say. "Or I can make myself scarce."

"It would be better if you were here in the living room with us. We're going to be discussing security for you."

"Look, I appreciate it, but I really don't need security."

He shakes his head. "I would feel better if you had it. It's a gut feeling, and my gut's rarely wrong. So humor me."

"Fine." I shrug. If some suited goons want to tail me to school and back, I'm not going to stop them.

"There's something else you should know—"

But then the elevator dings across the room, and someone steps out of it. Someone just as large as Jaxon, whose stare fixes me in place with the same kind of command and authority.

Jaxon continues, "Ryder is the guy you danced with at the club."

Fuck. Me.

Wait, he already did. With his fingers. While Jaxon was right in front of us, holding my throat, kissing me.

I didn't get a good look at Ryder's face that night. The lights were dim, and he was behind me. But he's just as breathtakingly handsome as Jaxon. His eyes are lighter, his hair slightly longer and a lighter brown. His body is just as big, just as muscular. My pussy tingles as I remember the feeling of being sandwiched between these two strong men.

I can't stop staring at him.

"Olivia," Jaxon is saying, and from the exasperated tone, I get the sense that he's said it a few times, trying to get my attention. Finally, he says sharply, "Babydoll."

I look away from Ryder and over to Jaxon, startled. Jaxon is smirking. I feel my face flush and I lift up a hand, hoping to cool my cheeks and hide their redness.

"Cute," Ryder says, but he's talking to Jaxon, not to me. "I can see why you brought her home."

A heavy pain works its way up my throat at his words. He's talking about me as if I'm not here, as if he didn't have his hands all over me last night, as if none of that meant anything at all to him.

It probably didn't.

And that hurts worst of all.

Ryder walks to the coffee table in front of me and sets down a folder of papers that I hadn't noticed he was holding. Jaxon picks them up and leafs through them.

"I want Terrence taking the lead," he says.

"Terrence is on the Velasquez detail," Ryder says.

"Then pull him off," Jaxon says. "I want him with Olivia."

Ryder folds his arm across his chest. "I hardly think we send out our best guy to protect her from an amateur stalker. The senator—"

"The senator will be fine with someone else on lead. Our men can run his detail in their sleep."

"Fine." Ryder puts his hands up in the air. "Terrence it is."

When he spins around and stalks back to the elevator, Jaxon says, "Where the hell do you think you're going?"

"Home."

"Stay here, asshole. It's late. I can use your help tomorrow."

I wish I was anywhere but in the middle of this. Jaxon said they were friends, but they seem to hate each other. But then Ryder turns back to us and his gaze lands on me, and I realize the truth. It isn't Jaxon he hates—it's me.

I gasp and fold my arms in front of me, trying to brace myself against the animosity swirling throughout the room.

Ryder sighs and looks away from me. He runs a hand through his hair. "Fine."

He's halfway to the hall when Jaxon says, "Olivia's sleeping in your usual room."

A door slams farther down the hall and I'm finally able to exhale. I can't believe I just witnessed that. I can't believe the guy who just had his fingers in my pussy less than forty-eight hours ago looked at me with such loathing, it was like I'm a household pest. A cockroach. My lungs feel squeezed empty of air. It's hard to breathe, and I pull my arms around myself more tightly.

"Olivia." Jaxon's voice is soft.

"I think—I think I'm ready for bed. Goodnight." I carefully set the art book down on the coffee table, keeping my gaze on the bright cover, which is starting to blur from the tears in my eyes.

"Olivia," he says again.

Standing up, I make my way toward the hall. Jaxon is suddenly in front of me, a wall of man. He reaches out and takes me into his arms.

"He's an asshole, I know," Jaxon says.

"He hates me," I whisper. "What did I do?"

Jaxon nudges my head up with a finger to my chin. "Absolutely nothing, except captivate him."

No, captivation is not at all what I witnessed just now. Disgust, disdain. Loathing.

"Don't cry, Babydoll," he says, then kisses my forehead. "My room is just across the hall."

He points to an open door, and I nod. "Thanks."

"You come get me if you need anything, okay?"

"Okay."

I can feel his gaze, heavy and hot as a brand on my back, as I go into my room and softly close the door behind me.

———

CONTINUE THE STORY IN *DADDIES' Babydoll*, the second episode in the serial! Click here to get it from your favorite retailer: https://books2read.com/babydoll-2

Confused about why the story isn't finished? Please re-read the Foreword at the front of this book, which explains it all, or re-read the book's description on the retailer where you purchased this volume.

ALSO BY CALISTA JAYNE

Fiercely Filthy Fairy Tales

Little Red's Temptation

Cinderella's Daddies

———

Their Babydoll

Daddies' Girl

Daddies' Babydoll

Daddies' Little Angel

Daddies' Princess

Daddies' Sweetheart

Daddies Ever After

ABOUT THE AUTHOR

Calista Jayne adores filthy, smutty romances featuring dominant-yet-tender men. When not writing or reading, she's falling in love with the heroes in K-dramas or walking along a California beach.

Manufactured by Amazon.ca
Bolton, ON

34913475R00069